This book
was donated
to the
Lowell School
Library
by

ABBY & AMALYA JOHNSON

2000

bell hooks

Happy to Be Nappy

Chris Raschka

 Jump at the Sun/Hyperion Books for Children • New York

First Edition
1 3 5 7 9 10 8 6 4 2

Library of Congress Cataloging-in-Publication Data
hooks, bell.
Happy to be nappy / by bell hooks:
illustrated by Chris RaschKa.—1st ed.
p.   cm.
Summary: Celebrates the joy and beauty of nappy hair.
ISBN 0-7868-0427-0 (trade)—0-7868-2377-1 (lib.)
[1. Hair—Fiction. 2. Afro-Americans—Fiction]
I. Raschka, Chris, ill. II. Title.
PZ7.H7663Hap 1999
[E]-dc21   97-50441

to Loving Ourselves —
bell hooks

To all the girlpies
who sweeten my life
and to the sweetest
of the sweet
my nieces,
Katrese and Sarah
—b.h.

**for Carol
— C.R.**

Girlpie hair smells clean

and sweet

is soft like cotton,
flower petal billowy soft,

full of frizz and fuzz.

A halo — a crown —

a covering for heads
that are round.

It can be smooth or patted down

pulled tight, cut close

or just let go

so wind can carry it

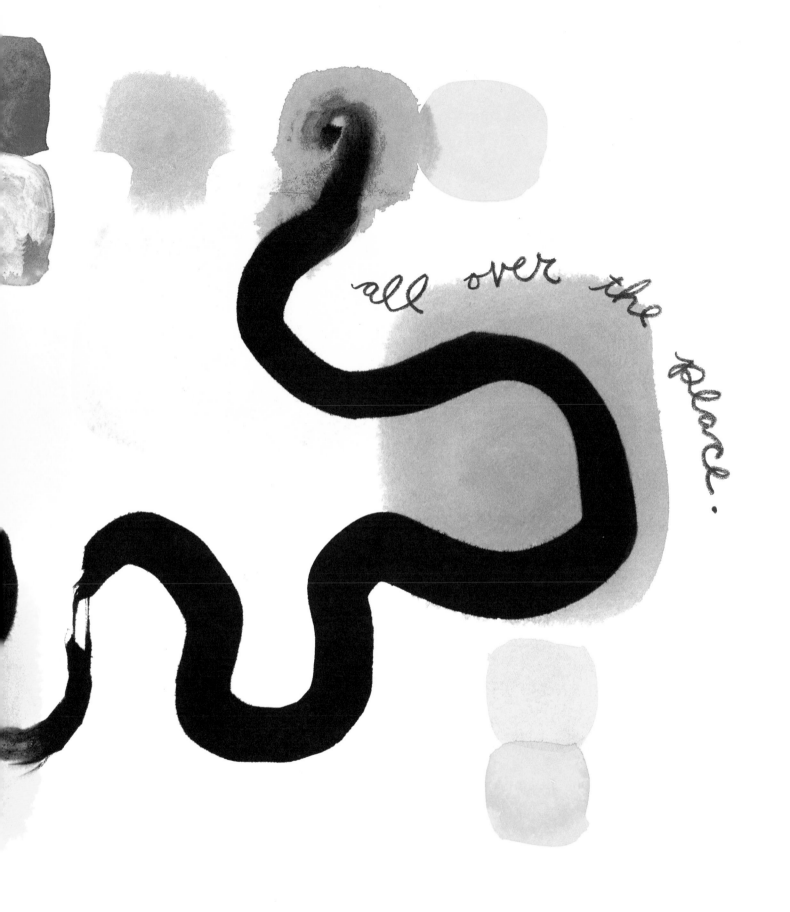

all over the place.

Hair to comb, hair to brush,

to twist and plait or just lie flat.

Hair for hands

to touch and play!

Hair to take the gloom away.

sitting still for hands to brush or braid

and make the day start hopefully.

All kinks gone!

All heads of joy!

These short tight naps

or plaited strands all

let girls go running free.

Happy with hair
all short and strong.

Happy with locks that twist and curl.

Just all girl happy!

Happy to be nappy hair!